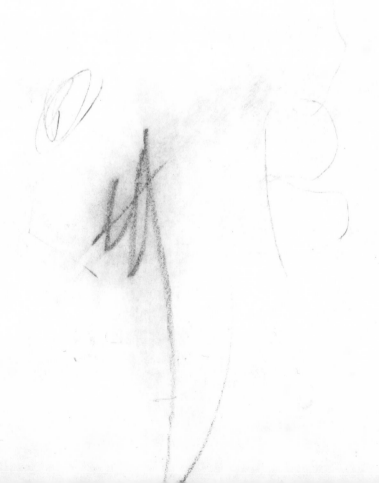

Squirrel's *Adventure*

in Alphabet Town

by *Laura Alden*
illustrated by Judi Collins

created by Wing Park Publishers

CHILDRENS PRESS®
CHICAGO

Library of Congress Cataloging-in-Publication Data

Alden, Laura, 1955-
    Squirrel's adventure in Alphabet Town / by Laura Alden ;
illustrated by Judi Collins.
       p.   cm. — (Read around Alphabet Town)
    Summary: Squirrel enjoys her Saturday at the seashore with
her sister.
    ISBN 0-516-05419-8
    [1. Alphabet.   2. Squirrels—Fiction.   3. Seashore—Fiction.]
I. Collins, Judi, ill.   II. Title.   III. Series.
PZ7.A3586Sq   1992
[E]—dc 20   92-1314
                                         CIP
                                         AC

Squirrel's *Adventure*

in Alphabet Town

You are now entering Alphabet Town,
With houses from "A" to "Z."
I'm going on an "S" adventure today,
So come along with me.

This is the "S" house of Alphabet
Town. Squirrel lives here.

Squirrel likes everything that starts
with the letter ''s.''

Squirrel loves Saturdays.

Sunday
Monday
Tuesday
Wednesday
Thursday
Friday
★ Saturday
seashore

This Saturday Squirrel is going
to the seashore with her sister.

She puts on her new

sweatsuit

and her new

sneakers.

Size 6

Next she makes

sandwiches

to take along for supper.

Then she packs a

suitcase

with clothes for the seashore.

Squirrel looks outside. The sun is shining. She sees her sister's car coming down the street—

pulling a new

sailboat!

"What a surprise!" says Squirrel.

Squirrel and her sister sing silly songs all the way to the seashore.

They stop only once—to stretch and to play on

swings

and a

slide.

At last Squirrel sees the sea.
Squirrel puts on her

swimming suit.

SPLASH! Squirrel jumps in the water.
She swims...

and swims and swims.

Then Squirrel and her sister build

castles
of sand.

They look for

shells.

Squirrel even finds a starfish.

Soon it is time for supper. Squirrel and her sister share

six sandwiches

and

seven soda pops.

"Let's go sailing," says Squirrel's sister. And away they sail.

Squirrel sees a

ship

way out in the sea.

Suddenly the sun stops shining. The sky gets dark.

Squirrel sees a storm coming. "Turn back!" she squeals.

The sailboat reaches the shore just in time. They are safe!

Squirrel feels just a little seasick.

Now there are lots of stars in the sky. Squirrel feels better. But she is sleepy.

It is time to go home. Squirrel
smiles to herself. It has been an
extra special Saturday.

MORE FUN WITH SQUIRREL

What's in a Name?

In my "s" adventure, you read many "s" words. My name begins with an "S." Many of my friends' names begin with "S" too. Here are a few.

Sam   Susan   Steve   Scarlett

Sharon   Steffie   Stacy   Stan

Do you know other names that start with "S"?
Does your name start with "S"?

Squirrel's Word Hunt

I like to hunt for "s" words. Can you help me find the words on this page that begin with "s"? How many are there? Can you read them?

soap

kiss

salad

nose

glass

soup

lipstick

lamb

Can you find any words with "s" in the middle?
Can you find any with "s" at the end?
Can you find a word with no "s"?

Squirrel's Favorite Things

"S" is my favorite letter. I love "s" things. Can you guess why? You can find some of my favorite "s" things in my house on page 7. How many "s" things can you find there? Can you think of more "s" things?

Now you make up an "s" adventure.

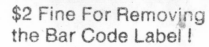